W9-DDA-165

Can Science Solve?

The Mystery
of the
Death of the
Dinosaurs

Chris Oxlade

Heinemann Library
Chicago, Illinois

Designed by AMR
Illustrations by Art Construction
Origination by Ambassador Litho Ltd.
Printed in China

06 05 04
10 9 8 7 6 5 4

Library of Congress Cataloging-in-Publication Data
Oxlade, Chris.
 The mystery of the death of the dinosaurs / Chris Oxlade.
    p. cm. -- (Can science solve?)
Includes bibliographical references and index.
Summary: Examines the disappearance of the dinosaurs and the various theories that exist to explain it.
  ISBN 1-58810-664-0 (lib.bdg.)   ISBN 1-58810-931-3 (pbk. bdg.)
 1. Dinosaurs--Juvenile literature. 2. Extinction (Biology)--Juvenile literature. [1. Dinosaurs. 2. Extinction (Biology)] I. Title. II. Series.
 QE861.5 .O85 2002
 567.9--dc21
                        2001004540

Acknowledgments
The author and publishers are grateful to the following for permission to reproduce copyright material:
Corbis, pp. 4, 15; Mary Evans Picture Library, pp. 6, 7; Science Photo Library, pp. 8, 10, 13, 14, 17, 18, 20, 23, 24, 25, 26, 29; J Sibbick/Natural History Museum, p. 11; Will & Dent McIntyre, p. 19; Oxford Scientific Films, p. 27; Bruce Coleman Collection, p. 28.

Cover photograph reproduced with permission of Science Photo Library.

Every effort has been made to contact copyright holders of any material reproduced in this book. Any omissions will be rectified in subsequent printings if notice is given to the publisher.

Some words are shown in bold, **like this.** You can find out what they mean by looking in the glossary.

Contents

Unsolved Mysteries

For centuries, people have been puzzled and fascinated by mysterious places, creatures, and events. Is there really a monster in Loch Ness? Did the lost city of Atlantis ever exist? Are crop circles messages from aliens, or simply clever hoaxes? Is there life on Mars or Venus? Why did the dinosaurs suddenly die out?

Some of these mysteries have baffled scientists, who have spent years trying to find the answers. But just how far can science go? Can it really explain the unexplained? Are there some mysteries that science simply cannot solve? Read on, and try to make up your own mind . . .

When you stand next to a dinosaur skeleton, it seems amazing that such huge animals could have lived on Earth.

This book tells you about the death of the dinosaurs. It looks at what the dinosaurs were; when, where, and how they lived; and how we know about them. Then it examines the theories about why they died.

When did the dinosaurs live?

Dinosaurs were an amazing group of animals. Some of the dinosaurs were the largest animals that have ever lived on land, weighing up to twenty times as much as an elephant. They dominated the world for more than 160 million years. That is more than 100 times longer than humans have existed. That is why it is such a mystery that, 65 million years ago, the dinosaurs completely disappeared. Every dinosaur alive at the time died.

What caused the death of these animals? It is a natural question to ask, but it is not an easy one to answer. The dinosaurs died out a very long time ago, so finding the answer means trying to discover what happened in the distant past. Some people think the dinosaurs were wiped out by a massive **meteorite** and the harsh winter conditions that followed. Others think they just died out naturally.

Without science, we would not even know that the dinosaurs existed. What steps are scientists taking in hopes of finding out why they disappeared? This book will help you to answer that question.

Beginnings of a Mystery

Two hundred years ago, nobody knew that the dinosaurs, or hundreds of other **extinct** species, ever existed. So they had no idea that these amazing creatures suddenly died out. Scientists also thought that Earth was a few thousand years old at most.

Early finds

People have been finding dinosaur bones for hundreds of years. The first find of a dinosaur **fossil** that we know about comes from 1677, when Robert Plot of Oxford University in England was sent a piece of a large thigh bone to examine. He thought it came from an elephant brought to Great Britain by the Romans, or from an extremely large human. We now know that it came from a dinosaur called *Megalosaurus*.

British scientist Sir Richard Owen (1804-1892) built some of the first dinosaur models.

The first scientific studies of dinosaurs were made in the 1820s. Gideon Mantell, a British doctor, found some large fossil teeth and bones. He concluded that they came from a giant **reptile,** which he named *Iguanodon.* William Buckland of Oxford University also studied some fossil bones. He figured out that they must have come from a huge, meat-eating reptile that he named *Megalosaurus,* meaning "giant lizard." These scientists had no reason to believe that similar animals were not still living in some unexplored part of the world.

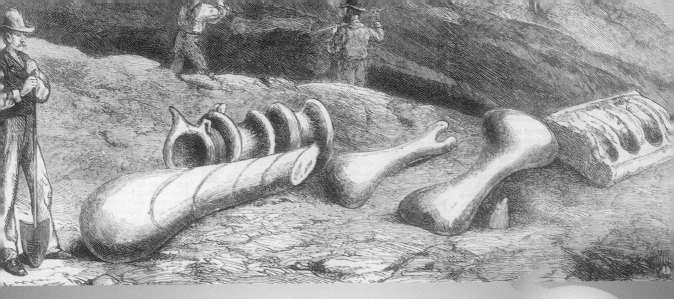

In the 1840s, another British scientist, Richard Owen, studied all the fossils of large reptiles found at the time. He found many similar features and reached the important conclusion that they all belonged to one group of reptiles that no longer lived on Earth. He gave the group the name *Dinosauria,* meaning "terrifying lizards." Soon there was great interest in dinosaurs.

This is an artist's impression of a dinosaur dig in the 19th century.

How old were the fossils?

At the same time, **geologists** were realizing that the rocks they studied must be extremely old. They saw huge mountains slowly **eroding** to form **sediment** and new rocks forming as the sediment fell to the bottom of rivers and lakes. They concluded that thick beds of **sedimentary rocks** must have taken millions of years to form. This meant that the fossils found in them must have come from creatures that lived millions of years ago.

In the early twentieth century, scientists devised a way of calculating the exact age of rocks. It worked by measuring how **radioactive** the rocks were. No dinosaur fossils were found in rocks younger than 65 million years, meaning that no dinosaurs existed after that time. So what had happened to the dinosaurs?

7

Measuring Time

Before we can look at the theories about why the dinosaurs died, we need to understand more about how they lived and what Earth was like at the time. This was a very long time ago, so first we need to understand how **geologists** and **paleontologists** measure time in the distant past and learn some of the terms they use.

The beginning of life

Earth is very, very old. According to many scientists, it was formed about 4.6 billion years ago from dust and gas left over after the sun formed. At first Earth was just a red-hot rock. Life is thought to have started from chemicals in the oceans about 3.5 billion years ago. For billions of years, the only forms of life were very simple single-celled organisms.

About 550 million years ago, more complicated forms of plants and animals **evolved.** Some forms started to colonize the land. The dinosaurs evolved about 225 million years ago and died out 65 million years ago. Humans evolved within the last 1.6 million years. We have been on Earth for only a tiny fraction of its life.

This is a trilobite fossil. It would have lived in the sea about 550 million years ago.

Geological time

Geologists and paleontologists use a geological timeline. They have divided the time since the formation of Earth into chunks and given each one a name. Each one begins and ends when the **fossils** from the time show that a major change took place on Earth.

Geological time is divided into two huge chunks called eons—the Precambrian and Phanerozoic. The Phanerozoic is divided into three eras. The Paleozoic era was when life lived mainly in the seas. The Mesozoic era was when the dinosaurs ruled. The Cenozoic era stretches from the death of the dinosaurs to the present day. Each of these eras is divided into smaller chunks called periods. The Mesozoic period, when the dinosaurs lived, is divided into the Triassic, Jurassic and Cretaceous periods.

The KT boundary

*The dinosaurs died out around the end of the Cretaceous period and the beginning of the Tertiary period, which was the first period in the Cenozoic era. This time is known as the **KT boundary**—K stands for "Cretaceous" (because C is used for the "Carboniferous" period) and T stands for "Tertiary."*

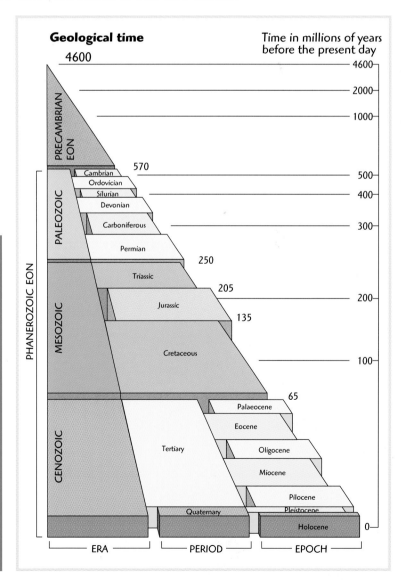

What Were the Dinosaurs Like?

Dinosaurs were **reptiles.** They shared some of the characteristics of lizards, crocodiles, snakes, and other modern reptiles. For example, we think dinosaurs had tough, scaly skin and their young hatched out of eggs. But there was one important difference. All dinosaurs had legs that came straight down from their bodies, rather than out and then down like the legs of modern-day lizards and crocodiles. Dinosaurs stood upright and walked either on two legs or four.

How many species?

So far, **paleontologists** have identified about 700 different species, or types, of dinosaurs. This is not very many, considering that there are thousands of species of birds and mammals alive today. There are probably hundreds more dinosaur species waiting to be discovered. Not all these species lived at the same time. Different species were constantly **evolving** and dying out during the 160 million years that the dinosaurs lived on Earth.

This artist's impression shows Earth during the Cretaceous period.

Big and small

Dinosaurs are famous for their massive size. It is true that some dinosaurs were staggeringly big. Animals such as *Diplodocus* grew up to 74 feet (27 meters) long and weighed 70 or 80 tons. That is twice as long and as heavy as a fully-loaded eighteen-wheeler truck. But many species of dinosaurs were no bigger than cats or dogs, and some were as small as chickens. Some dinosaurs had armored plates in their skin and weapons on their tails for self-defense. Not all dinosaurs were fierce **carnivores,** either. Many were **herbivores.**

The carnivore Tyrannosaurus *evolved during the Cretaceous period.*

Evolution of the dinosaurs

At the end of Palaeozoic era, 250 million years ago, there were no dinosaurs. The land was ruled by other types of reptiles. These reptiles evolved into turtles, another group of small reptiles, and a group of reptiles called the **archosaurs.** The archosaurs evolved into different groups, too, including marine reptiles, flying reptiles (called pterosaurs), crocodiles, and the first dinosaurs.

By the end of the Triassic period, 205 million years ago, the early dinosaurs had evolved into many groups, and they dominated the land. Their **evolution** continued for another 140 million years. Some dinosaur species became rare or died out completely and new ones evolved. By the end of the Cretaceous period, horned and duck-billed dinosaurs were the most common.

The Dinosaurs' World

The dinosaurs dominated the world for a long time, so it is not surprising that it changed a great deal during that time. When the dinosaurs first **evolved** in the Triassic period, there was just one big land mass called Pangaea, which means "all earth." Since then, Pangaea has gradually split apart, creating the continents that we know today. Most of this land movement took place when the dinosaurs were alive, and it had a huge effect on the conditions on Earth.

Over millions of years, Pangaea split apart to form the continents we know today.

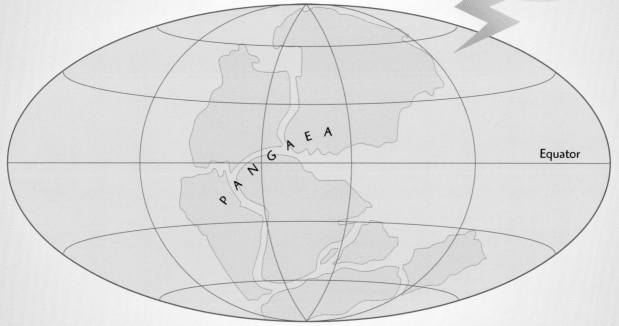

Equator

Changing climates

Climate is the pattern of weather that a place has. The world's climates have always changed slowly, with periods of warmer climates and then cooler climates. During the time that the dinosaurs lived, the climates changed as Pangaea split up. The drifting continents affected the climates of the whole planet, and each piece of land slowly moved through different climates.

Pterosaurs were flying reptiles. They died out at the same time as the dinosaurs.

In the middle of the Cretaceous period, Earth was very warm, with **subtropical** conditions almost everywhere. Even though it was completely dark for months on end, forests grew on land near Earth's north and south poles, which have ice caps today. Then, toward the end of the Cretaceous, the climate started to cool again. Sea levels began to fall, as sea water froze and became part of the ice caps, and some places started to have regular seasons.

Changing plants

When the dinosaurs first appeared, plants were very different from today. They were mostly ferns and mosses. There were no flowering plants. During the Jurassic period, conifers evolved into pines, redwoods, and monkey puzzle trees, forming huge forests. By the Cretaceous period, flowering plants dominated the plant world, as they do today. The plant-eating dinosaurs had to adjust to eating the new plants that evolved.

Other animals

*Dinosaurs were not the only animals that lived on Earth at the time. There were many other species of **reptiles,** such as the flying pterosaurs and the swimming ichthyosaurs and plesiosaurs. There were also fish, birds, small furry mammals, and insects. Many of these were prey for the smaller **carnivorous,** or meat-eating, dinosaurs.*

Fossil Evidence

We know for certain that dinosaurs existed, because we have found their remains. We also have found the remains of other animals and plants from the same time period. These remains are called **fossils.** They give us clues about how dinosaurs lived and what their world was like. Fossils have been found in every continent on Earth.

What are fossils?

Fossils form when the remains of an animal or plant become buried under **sediment,** such as mud or **silt.** The soft parts of an animal rot away, leaving only the bones and teeth. In the wet sediment, **minerals** replace the bones and teeth over time, turning them into rock. Over millions of years, the remains turn into rock such as sandstone. As the surface **erodes,** the fossil is exposed and is likely to be found.

Dinosaur skeletons usually are found in many pieces and have to be put back together.

Information from fossils

Fossils can tell scientists a lot of details about a dinosaur. Fossil bones allow **paleontologists** to work out the size and shape of the animal and how it moved. Fossil footprints tell us that some dinosaurs walked on two legs. Rare fossil eggs have been found in groups, which tells us that some dinosaurs lived in groups, like seabirds do today. Fossil skin, which rarely is found, tells us what dinosaurs looked like.

But fossils cannot tell us everything. Only a small number of all the animals that die turn into fossils. Scientists think we only have fossils of about one percent of all the types of animals that have lived on Earth. There are many gaps in what paleontologists call the fossil record. There may have been hundreds of species of dinosaurs about which we will never learn.

This fossilized dinosaur footprint was found in New Mexico.

More evidence

Fossils of plants from the dinosaur age tell us how Earth looked then and how the climate changed over time. Matching fossils from different continents tells us how the supercontinent of Pangaea fit together.

The Dinosaur Extinction

If an animal or plant is said to be **extinct,** that means that all the individual animals or plants in that species have died. The species will never live again. Throughout the history of life on Earth—from 3.5 billion years ago to the present day—millions of species have **evolved** and have become extinct. **Fossil** records show us that very few species have existed for more than a million years. In fact, 99 percent of all the species that have ever lived on Earth are now extinct.

Adapt or die

Species normally become extinct because environmental conditions change. For example, a species that lives only in a certain area could die out as its **habitat** gradually turns to desert or because a new species of **predator** evolves and feeds on it. These changes normally take millions of years. Some species naturally evolve or adapt to living in the new conditions, perhaps turning into completely new species. Others do not evolve quickly enough and die out.

Fossil records also show that there are periods in geological time when thousands of species have died out in a very short space of time. **Paleontologists** call these periods extinction events or mass extinctions.

The KT-boundary event

The most significant mass extinction happened at the **KT boundary,** between the Cretaceous and Tertiary periods. Paleontologists call it the KT-boundary event. Every species of dinosaur that was alive at the time died.

Unfortunately, we cannot date rocks accurately enough to tell how long the KT-boundary event lasted. Some scientists think it lasted as little as a few days, while others think it lasted for more than a million years. So although people say that the dinosaurs all died at exactly the same time, we cannot prove that this was the case.

Other species that died

It was not only the dinosaurs that died out during the KT-boundary event. Many other creatures died too, including some species of lizards, sharks, and birds. All species of plesiosaurs and mesosaurs became extinct. So did the ammonites, which had lived in the oceans for hundreds of millions of years. In fact, about 75 percent of all the animal species died. Those that survived included most species of fish, amphibians, and mammals.

This is a skeleton of a dinosaur that lived in the oceans on Earth more than 65 million years ago. It is over 21 feet (8 meters) long.

The Impact Theory

The first and most famous theory about what caused the death of the dinosaurs is that conditions were changed dramatically by a massive **meteorite** smashing into Earth. This is called the extraterrestrial impact theory or catastrophic theory.

A meteorite is a piece of space debris that lands on Earth. Some meteorites are made of rock, some are made mainly of iron, and some are a mixture of the two. The pieces of debris are left over from the formation of the **solar system.** Hundreds of pieces of debris collide with Earth every day. Most are very small and burn up as they enter Earth's **atmosphere** at speeds of up to 43 miles (70 kilometers) per second. On occasion, larger pieces get through the atmosphere and create impact **craters.**

When a large meteorite landed in Siberia in 1908 it flattened trees for many miles around.

18

Collision effects

What would have happened if a huge meteorite had hit Earth at the time of the dinosaurs? Here is the theory: The meteorite was very large, probably at least 6.2 miles (10 kilometers) across—the same size as a major town. It came down through the atmosphere at 31 miles (50 kilometers) per second, leaving a bright streak across the sky, and smashed into the shallow sea.

The impact caused an explosion equal to 100 million billion tons of dynamite going off at once. That is an explosion more powerful than if all the world's nuclear weapons went off at the same time. It made a crater more than 6.2 miles (10 kilometers) deep and hundreds of miles across. A powerful shock wave blasted out from the site, setting forests on fire. Giant waves spread across the sea, flooding low-lying coastal areas for thousands of miles.

The impact, shock wave, and flooding would have killed thousands of dinosaurs. But scientists believe that most died because of the climate change that followed.

An impact winter

The meteorite impact threw millions of tons of dust high into Earth's atmosphere. This dust slowly spread around the upper atmosphere, creating a dusty blanket that blocked out the sun's heat and light. Over the next few months, the atmosphere cooled by as much as 68°F (20°C). The weather became very cold, and plants could not grow properly. Acid rain fell from the clouds. The dinosaurs could never survive these conditions.

Meteorite Evidence

There is evidence that a huge **meteorite** hit Earth at the end of the Cretaceous period. Layers of rock formed at the time contain chemicals that could have come from a meteorite, and a huge **crater** has been found just off the coast of Mexico. This evidence supports the impact theory.

The iridium anomaly

Iridium is a type of metal. Only tiny amounts of it are found in the rocks of Earth's crust, but meteorites often contain a lot of it. In several places around the world, **geologists** have found a layer of **sedimentary rock,** called mudstone, that contains much higher levels of iridium than in other rocks. They call this layer the iridium **anomaly.** Using **radiometric** techniques, the mudstone has been found to be about 65 million years old. That means it formed at the end of the Cretaceous period, on the **KT boundary,** around the same time as the dinosaurs died out.

The Arizona Crater, formed 22,000 years ago, is obvious proof that big meteorites have hit Earth in the past.

It is thought that a meteorite impact would have thrown dust rich in iridium into the **atmosphere,** which was then spread around the world. The dust eventually fell with rain and was washed down rivers and deposited in the bottom of lakes and seas, eventually forming the layer of iridium-rich rock.

Finding a crater

You can see from Earth that the surface of the moon is covered in impact craters. Most of these were formed billions of years ago when meteorites hit the moon. As many meteorites must have hit Earth, but there are only a few impact craters visible and none large enough to have been caused by a meteorite 6.2 miles (10 kilometers) across. Most craters have disappeared because they have **eroded** away or have been covered by new rock.

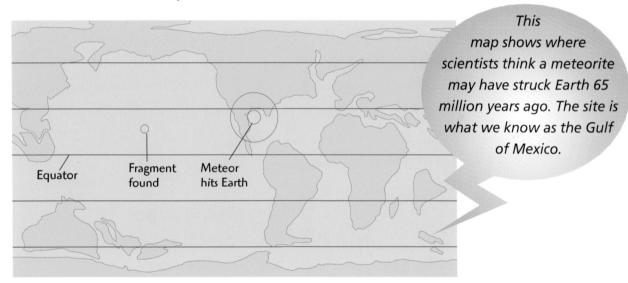

Equator

Fragment found

Meteor hits Earth

This map shows where scientists think a meteorite may have struck Earth 65 million years ago. The site is what we know as the Gulf of Mexico.

But in the late 1990s, evidence was found of a vast crater, 149 miles (240 kilometers) wide, hidden under rocks on the Yucatan peninsula in Mexico. Named the Chicxulub Crater, it is in rocks formed in the late Cretaceous period. Rocks within a few hundred miles of the site contain a layer of tiny balls of glass that would have been formed by the intense heat of a meteorite impact. Was this crater formed by the meteorite that killed the dinosaurs?

The Habitat Loss Theory

The second main theory about the death of the dinosaurs is that they died out over millions of years because their **habitats** changed slowly and they could not adapt quickly enough to survive in the conditions. This is called the habitat loss theory or gradualist theory.

Fossil records show that many species of dinosaurs were dying out in the last 10 million years of the Cretaceous period. The numbers of individual skeletons of each species found from this period show that this was the case. The number of different species was also declining.

Changing conditions

At the end of the Cretaceous period, the world's climate was slowly cooling. Sea levels were falling after being very high in the middle of the Cretaceous period. These two factors led to a change in habitat for the dinosaurs.

Away from the equator, the lush vegetation began to be replaced by trees, and year-round warm weather was replaced by seasons with cold winters. The shallow seas near the coasts became land, and the land that was near the sea turned drier. The **herbivores** could no longer find the right food to eat. They began to die out. The **carnivores,** which ate the herbivores, went hungry. The dinosaurs also had to fight other animals for food. All these changes were very slow. They took millions of years to happen.

The volcanic eruption of Mount St. Helens in Washington sends a cloud of ash, gas, and rock into the atmosphere.

Volcanic activity

Another theory is that the climate change happened quickly, perhaps over thousands rather than millions of years, and was caused by volcanic activity.

In India, there is a huge deposit of basalt called the Deccan Traps. Volcanoes must have been erupting there for tens of thousands of years to produce such a huge amount of basalt. It is thought that volcanoes formed when the drifting continents caused India to crash slowly into Asia. This happened at the time the dinosaurs died out. Eruptions on this scale would have sent gas and dust into the **atmosphere,** causing a climate change.

23

More Extinction Theories

We have looked at the two main theories that try to explain the death of the dinosaurs. They are the impact theory and the **habitat** loss theory. These two theories are sometimes called the bang and whimper theories. But there are dozens of other theories about why the dinosaurs died out, and hundreds of scientific papers have been written on the subject. Some of the theories are based on scientific evidence, but others are just plain silly.

Star activity

Two **extinction** theories have to do with the sun and other stars. One is that the sun cooled down for a period of time, reducing the amount of heat reaching Earth. This led to global cooling, which in turn led to **climate** change and the death of the dinosaurs. The other is that a nearby star exploded, causing a **supernova** that sent waves of deadly radiation toward Earth.

A supernova happens when a star many times bigger than the sun comes to the end of its life.

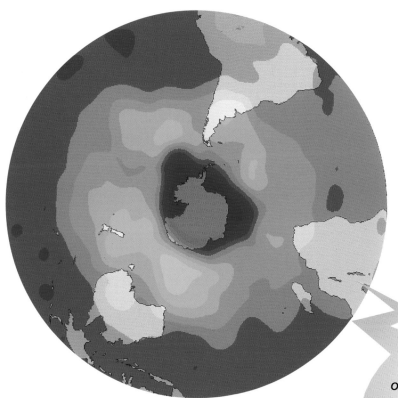

Disease and illness

There are also theories that the dinosaurs died out because of some sort of disease or illness. Perhaps the disease was a plague that spread when sea levels fell, allowing dinosaurs that had **evolved** on different continents to meet and spread the disease.

More theories

Another theory is that plant-eating dinosaurs created huge amounts of **methane** gas. Big dinosaurs would have eaten hundreds of pounds of plants every day and would have passed a lot of gas! This extra methane in the **atmosphere** would have damaged the **ozone layer,** which in turn would have caused changes in climate and vegetation that threatened the lives of dinosaurs. Other theories are that the dinosaurs died because of competing with caterpillars for plants to eat or that mammals ate all their eggs.

Some of these theories are possible, but there is no firm evidence for any of them.

25

Extinction Through History

The **KT-boundary** event, in which the dinosaurs were wiped out, was not the only time in history when hundreds of species became **extinct** in a short amount of time. There seem to have been several mass extinctions since the time advanced life developed about 550 million years ago.

Fossil records show a regular pattern of mass extinctions, about every 26 million years for the last 250 million years. Five of these mass extinctions have been on a huge scale, when more than half of all the species alive at the time were killed off. Regular mass extinctions could be caused by some regular astronomical event, such as Earth's orbit around the sun taking it across the path of a cloud of asteroids or comets.

The Permian extinction

The greatest mass extinction of all time happened at the end of the Permian period. It is called the Permian event, and it was catastrophic. About 95 percent of all the species living at the time were wiped out.

After the world had recovered, new species **evolved** from those that were left. These included the early dinosaurs, who took advantage of the lack of competition from other species.

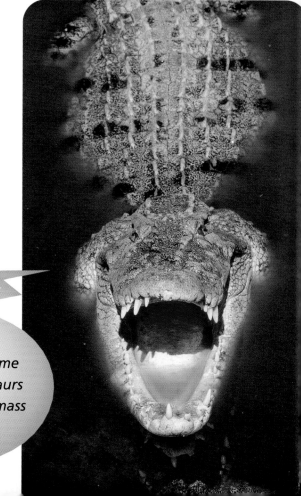

Crocodiles evolved at the same time as the dinosaurs but survived two mass extinctions.

Another extinction, this time not quite so large, separates the Triassic and Jurassic periods. This left the world ready to be dominated by the dinosaurs. So it is likely that the dinosaurs, who were killed off in a mass extinction, had only become successful because of another mass extinction.

The coelacanth has been on Earth for about 400 million years. It was thought to be extinct until 1932, when one was caught.

A modern extinction?

There is no reason to think that there will not be another mass extinction in the future. A few decades ago, a **meteorite** *impact was thought to be something that only happened in the distant past. But in the last few years, the world's governments have begun to take the idea seriously. Organizations have been set up to watch for any large asteroids coming too close to Earth. Whether we could stop one before it landed is for scientists to work out.*

In Conclusion

So can science really solve the mystery of the death of the dinosaurs? It is not an easy job, because scientists have to find out what happened millions of years ago and they have only rocks to study.

Science tells us that the dinosaurs died in a relatively short period of time, compared to how long they lived on Earth. It also tells us that it is likely that a giant **meteorite** landed on Earth and that the climate was cooling. But science cannot tell us just how quickly the dinosaurs died out, or whether it was a meteorite impact or **climate** change that actually killed them.

Even the experts cannot be sure how the dinosaurs died. Most think that one of the two main theories—the impact theory or the **habitat** loss theory—could be correct, or that the dinosaurs were slowly dying out before they were finished off by a meteorite.

What is certain is that there is plenty more to find out. We only know a tiny fraction of what there is to know about the dinosaurs. Our knowledge is getting better all the time as new **fossils** are found. Perhaps proof for one of the theories will be found soon.

*The tuatara is a species of **reptile** that has survived since the Jurassic period. Could some dinosaurs have survived, too?*

What do you think?

Now that you have read about the scientific investigations into the death of the dinosaurs, can you draw any conclusions?

Do you think that one of the two main theories is more likely than the other? Perhaps you prefer the impact theory because it is more exciting. What about some of the other theories? Do you think you can dismiss them just because they seem unlikely? Remember, there is no evidence to say they are not true. Do you have any theories of your own about what killed the dinosaurs?

Try to keep an open mind. Remember that if scientists throughout history had not bothered to investigate things that appeared to be strange or mysterious, many scientific discoveries may never have been made.

*Bits of space dust fall through Earth's **atmosphere** every day, causing shooting stars. Did a big lump of rock from space wipe out the dinosaurs?*

Glossary

anomaly   something that is out of the ordinary or unusual

archosaurs   group of reptiles that lived about 250 million years ago and were ancestors of dinosaurs

atmosphere   blanket of gas that surrounds Earth

carnivore   animal that eats only meat. Dinosaurs that eat meat are called carnivorous.

climate   weather conditions

crater   wide, dish-shaped hole in the surface of a planet or moon, made when a meteorite crashes into the surface

erode   to wear away by the actions of flowing water, wind, or ice

evolution   development of a species of animal or plant

evolve   to gradually develop a new species of animal and plant over millions of years

extinct   no longer living. *Extinction* describes the condition of being extinct.

fossil   remains of an animal or plant that has changed into rock after millions of years

geologist   person who studies the rocks of Earth's crust

habitat   place where a species of animal or plant lives

herbivore   animal that eats only plants

KT boundary   time at the end of the Cretaceous period and the beginning of the Tertiary period, about 65 million years ago

methane   gas that occurs underground and also is made when plants rot or are digested by animals

meteorite   piece of rock from space that comes through Earth's atmosphere and hits the ground

minerals   chemicals from which rocks are made

ozone layer layer of the gas ozone (a form of oxygen) in the upper atmosphere that keeps harmful ultraviolet radiation from reaching Earth's surface

paleontologist person who studies fossils

predator animal that hunts other animals for food

radioactive giving off energy particles

radiometric way of finding the age of a piece of rock by measuring the amount of radiation coming from it

reptile cold-blooded animal with scaly skin

sediment mud, sand, and small pieces of rock that are washed down a river and then settle on the riverbed or seabed

sedimentary rocks rocks that are formed when layers of sediment are buried deep underground

silt sediment that is made of very tiny particles of rock

solar system our sun and the planets and moons that orbit it

subtropical warm climate with dry seasons followed by seasons of heavy rain

supernova massive explosion that happens when a large star comes to the end of its life

Further Reading

Oxlade, Chris. *The Mystery of Black Holes.* Chicago, Heinemann Library, 1999.

Wallace, Holly. *The Mystery of the Abominable Snowman.* Chicago: Heinemann Library, 1999.

Wallace, Holly. *The Mystery of the Loch Ness Monster.* Chicago: Heinemann Library, 1999.

Index